This book is dedicated to every child who lives with type 1 diabetes (T1D). Thanks to some remarkable kids, their inspiring stories, and a different way of thinking, T1D doesn't have to get in the way of living their best lives.

The people who created this book:

Writers:
Kevin Speirs and Scott Wanderman

Art Directors:
Lucas Comins and Matthew Nieri

Illustrator:
John Mazzarella

Creative Direction:
Dina Peck and Michele Monteforte

Producers:
Samantha Ferrara and Jessica Chiang

T1D won't stop me!

Billy's a cool kid with an even COOLER ATITTUDE.

He's one of a kind and always does things his own special way. Like the time he rigged a pulley system to his blanket so he can make his bed quicker.

He also has type 1 diabetes, or as Billy likes to say, T1D. That means he has to take insulin to help turn food into energy, but he doesn't let it get in his way.

He lives every day by his motto:

T1D won't stop me!

2

Today is the **town fair,** and Billy can't wait to go.

He hopped out of bed and checked his blood sugar...

Too **HIGH** or too **LOW?**

103

That's the number for me!

4

A big day calls for a

BIG
BREAKFAST

Billy counted his carbs,
gave himself insulin,
and scarfed down his food.

He packed his backpack, along with **some snacks.**

He grabbed everything he needs for his T1D and was off,

"T1D won't stop me!"

On the way to the fair
he saw his friend **Katie**

sitting next to her bike
broken to bits.

Billy told her,

"Don't let a **broken bike**

stop you from getting where you need to go."

"Let's turn that **broken bike** into a UNICYCLE."

Using the good parts of the bike,

Billy and Katie made a spiffy

new unicycle. "Thanks, Billy!

You saved the day!"

"You got it, Katie. **T1D won't stop me!** And a broken bike won't stop you."

Down the road,
Billy saw
MR. LEE
trying to
water his garden.

But his hose
had a
BIG
OL'
HOLE.

11

"Mr. Lee, sometimes you just have to think a little differently.

"Don't let that

HOLEY HOSE

stop you from watering your garden. What if we turned your hose into a sprinkler?"

They poked a few holes
here and a few more there,
and Mr. Lee was able
to water his entire
garden at once.

"Thanks, Billy. What a

GREAT IDEA!"

As Billy walked past the
baseball field,
he saw his friend

TEDDY

looking sad
on the bench.

Teddy's arm was broken so he'd have to miss the rest of the season.

Billy remembered how important it is to be prepared, even for the unexpected.

Billy reached into his backpack and pulled out a **FUN FOAM FINGER.**

"T1D won't stop me!

And a broken arm shouldn't stop you.

"You can still help the team
by cheering them on
and being their biggest fan."

"THANKS, DUDE!"

Teddy gave him a high-five
with his good arm, of course,
and Billy was off.

Just then, Billy started to feel weird and shaky.

He felt **wobbly** and even a little **woobly.**

He knew it was time to check his blood sugar.

"Uh-oh! It's **low.** That's a **no-go.**"

But Billy
    had just the thing!

He pulled out his

trusty juice box

from his

backpack.

He drank the juice box
and rested for a bit.
After 15 minutes he checked his

blood SUGAR again.

Billy was feeling good
and back on his way.

21

Once again,
he cheered out loud,

Around the corner Billy saw his teacher

Mrs. Gomez

struggling with grocery bags.

Oranges, apples, peaches, and pears

bounced down the road!

"Oh, no!" she cried.
     "My bags are way too heavy.
I'm never going to make it
        all the way home."

24

Billy had just the answer!
He pulled out his
slick-riding skateboard
and a double-dutch
JUMP ROPE
from his backpack.

Billy shouted,
"Put your bags on my board
and use it as a cart!"
"A+ Billy!
This is a huge help!"

"T1D won't stop me! And all those GROCERIES won't stop you!"

26

Down the block Billy spotted a

in front of his friend
Susie's house.

So Billy ran over
and asked her
what was wrong.

"I'm moving and
I'm really sad.
I'm going to lose all
of my friends," Susie said.

Billy also felt sad and thought,
"Moving shouldn't stop you
from keeping your friends."

Billy said,
"We don't have to stop being

FRIENDS

just because you're in a new town."

Billy hugged
Susie.

"Don't be sad.
We'll still be friends
and keep in touch.
And guess what? You'll make more
friends in your new town."

DEAR, BILLY

I am writing to you ♥ ♥
because I misss you soooo
♥ much.

Double FRIENDS
for double FUN!

"You're right, Billy. You're the best."
Billy didn't say goodbye.
Instead he said,

**"See ya later,
ALLIGATOR."**

After his adventure-packed day,

Billy finally made it to the fair.

The entire town was there.

T O W N ★ F A I R

Billy knows that everyone has to deal with things that can get in the way, just like him. But...

being
prepared and
thinking
differently

can go a long, long way.
Just look at all the people
he helped today!

As Billy whizzed past
the cotton candy machine,
he heard someone yell,
"Oh, no! The ticket machine
stopped working!"

COTTON
CANDY $1 50

FAIR

He shouted, "T1D won't stop me!" and ran off to save the day.

The people who created this book:

Writers:
Kevin Speirs and Scott Wanderman

Art Directors:
Lucas Comins and Matthew Nieri

Illustrator:
John Mazzarella

Creative Direction:
Dina Peck and Michele Monteforte

Producers:
Samantha Ferrara and Jessica Chiang

Co-creators:
Amina Fadera, Dylan Elizabeth Wolski, Janelle Murray, Jillian McLeod, Sage Green, Samantha Lyons, Sean Bennett, Sophia Sharma, Zakaria Bogni, and Zoe Rhodes-Wolin.

JDRF

JDRF is the leading global organization funding type 1 diabetes research. Their mission is a world without type 1 diabetes.

Patients & Purpose

Patients & Purpose is an advertising agency dedicated to patients and health brands. Their focus is making patients better.

Made in the USA
Middletown, DE
25 January 2020